www.enchantedlionbooks.com

First Reprint Edition published in 2017 by Enchanted Lion Books,
67 West Street, 317A, Brooklyn, New York 11222
Copyright © 1959 by Jacqueline Ayer
Rights arranged with the estate of Jacqueline Ayer
Color restoration and layout: Marc Drumwright
Originally published in 1959 by Harcourt, Brace and Company, New York, New York
All rights reserved under International and Pan-American Copyright Conventions.
A CIP record is on file with the Library of Congress
Printed in China in February 2017 by RR Donnelley Asia Printing Solutions Limited
ISBN: 978-1-59270-224-4
1 3 5 7 9 8 6 4 2

The Paper-Flower Tree

The Paper-Flower Tree

Jacqueline Ayer

A Tale from Thailand

Enchanted Lion Books, New York

For
Sa-ad,
Chamlat,
Som,
Chawang,
Pi Tamruat

ONCE upon a time there was a little girl whose name was Miss Moon.
She lived in a little village that sat all alone, far from the city.
Under the enormous blue sky the rice fields stretched around it
for miles and miles and miles.

In the late afternoon, when the village was quiet,
the warm wind wandered over the fields.
Then Miss Moon would come with her baby brother
to watch the cars and the trucks pass by
on the road that came from the city.

One day, when the road was empty and silent
and the sun hung over it angry and hot,
Miss Moon saw a little man in the distance,
puffing and blowing as he walked slowly along.
He carried over his shoulder a bamboo stick,
on which were tied colored bits of paper
that fluttered in the wind.

"Where are you going, grandfather?" Miss Moon said
to the stranger as he came closer.
"I'm following the road, wherever it takes me;
that's where I'm going," the old man said.

"What is that marvelous thing that you carry?"
"Indeed, it is marvelous," the old man replied.
"This, little mouse, is a paper-flower tree!"

Miss Moon smiled. She loved the tree. It was then
she knew that she had to have one.

"How pretty it is!" she said to the old man. "All those paper flowers
twinkling in the sun. I wish I had a tree like that one."

"One copper coin will buy you two flowers. If one of them has a seed,"
the old man said, "who knows? Perhaps you can plant it—
perhaps you can grow a tree for yourself."

"But I haven't a copper coin," Miss Moon said sadly.
"Then," answered the old man, smiling, "I suppose I'll have to give
you a flower." And he gave her the smallest one. "See, little mouse,
this one has a seed," and he pointed to a little black bead on a string.
"Plant it—and perhaps it will grow. I make no promises.
Perhaps it will grow. Perhaps it will not."

Miss Moon thanked the old man. "Thank you for my tree."

"It's not a tree yet; it's only a flower, and a paper one at that,"
he replied as he waved goodbye.

Miss Moon planted her paper-flower seed deep in the earth.
She built a little thatched roof to shade it from the sun.
She waited and watched for the little seed to grow.

The rice fields changed from yellow to brown to a bright and beautiful green.
The people from the little village planted, transplanted, and gathered the rice.
Day followed day, sometimes sunny, sometimes green and rainy.
So many days made months and months, so many months
that a whole year went by.

Miss Moon waited and watched for the little seed to grow.
Everyone thought she was foolish.

"Miss Moon," they said.
"You can't possibly grow a tree from a bead."

"You're wasting your time. Whoever heard of a paper-flower tree!"

But Miss Moon remembered the tree and how beautiful it was. She would wait. She was sure it would grow.

One day, down the strip of black road,
came a rickety, rackety truck, tooting its horn
and churning up billows of dust.

It rolled right into the little village,
and—rickety, rackety, crash bam—it came to a stop.
A strange little brown man, dressed in flashy, raggy tatters,
hopped up like a bird to the top of the truck.

Waving his arms, he shouted to the crowd that gathered.
This is what he said:
"Here we are! Musicians and dancers; magicians and clowns!
For a few silver coins, we'll show you how clever we are."

Then, in the crowd, Miss Moon saw him—
the funny old man with his paper-flower tree.

"Old grandfather!" she called to him. "Do you remember me?
You gave me a flower from your tree."

"Well, well, little mouse," the old man said.
"Indeed, I remember you."

"Grandfather," she told him, "I've planted the seed from your paper-flower tree, just as you said, and I've waited and watched, but there's nothing come as yet."

The old man's face was sad for a moment. "But, little mouse, I never promised that it would grow. I only said it might grow. Perhaps it won't, and then again, perhaps it will."

That night, under the enormous night sky,
the dancers and clowns with chalk-white faces,
dressed in silks and crowns and in raggle-taggle-
baggy gowns, crowded on the little stage.

The tiny cymbals sang clap-stop, clap-stop.
The drums beat slowly—and then faster and faster—
for hours and hours till the moon went down.

Miss Moon fell asleep to dream happily of bright-light colors
and rice fields filled with paper-flower trees.

Early in the morning, Miss Moon was awakened by the familiar smell of the cooking fire. She got up to look at the new-sky day. And there it was—glowing in the morning sun, fluttering in the morning breeze—a paper-flower tree!

"Grandfather!" she shouted. "I've got my tree. My paper-flower tree!"

He smiled and waved as the old truck rumbled and roared away.
"Goodbye, little mouse!" he called.

When Miss Moon showed the villagers her tree, they said,
"Oh well, of course—those are the old man's paper flowers
on a stick. You can't grow a tree from a bead!"

But Miss Moon didn't care.
She didn't care at all.
They didn't think her tree was real.
She knew it was.

She was as happy as a little girl could be.
Miss Moon finally had a paper-flower tree.